P9-DND-854

BRAVE DOG
BLIZZARD

BRAVE DOG BLIZZARD

by Sharon Salisbury O'Toole

illustrated by Stella Ormai

A
LITTLE APPLE
PAPERBACK

SCHOLASTIC INC.
New York Toronto London Auckland Sydney

If you purchased this book without a cover, you should
be aware that this book is stolen property. It was reported
as "unsold and destroyed" to the publisher, and neither
the author nor the publisher has received any payment
for this "stripped book."

No part of this publication may be reproduced in whole or in
part, or stored in a retrieval system, or transmitted in any
form or by any means, electronic, mechanical, photocopying,
recording, or otherwise, without written permission of the
publisher. For information regarding permission, write to
Scholastic Inc., 730 Broadway, New York, NY 10003.

ISBN 0-590-44409-3

Text copyright © 1992 by Sharon Salisbury O'Toole.
Illustrations copyright © 1992 by Scholastic Inc.
All rights reserved. Published by Scholastic Inc.

12 11 10 9 8 7 6 5 4 3   2 3 4 5 6 7/9

Printed in the U.S.A.   28

First Scholastic printing, March 1992

This book is dedicated to
the talented writer and editor, Bridget O'Toole.

Contents

BRAVE DOG BLIZZARD

Chapter 1

Blizzard's Family

Blizzard jumped to his feet. "Woof! Woof!" he barked fiercely. Several sheep, who were grazing peacefully in the warm spring sunshine, lifted their heads and looked around nervously for their lambs. The baby sheep, worn out from a morning of playing, were napping in the shade of a big tree.

"It's okay, Blizzard," called a woman's voice. "It's only Rebecca and me."

The big white dog relaxed when he saw Mrs. Hancock and her daughter walking toward him. He was a Hungarian komondor, and his job was to protect the sheep on the Hancocks' ranch in Wyoming.

Like all sheep ranchers in Wyoming,

the Hancocks had to worry about coyotes, stray dogs, and other predators that attack sheep. Blizzard stayed with the flock day and night to protect the mother sheep — the ewes — and their lambs from danger.

He also warned the Hancocks with loud barking whenever a stranger approached. He had been trained by the Hancocks to be a guardian dog.

"Look," Rebecca said. "There's Libby." The silvery-gray ewe had been raised with Blizzard, and she seldom strayed far from her friend.

The big white dog wagged his tail and trotted over, leaving Libby behind. Mrs. Hancock and Rebecca were lugging a large bag of dry dog food. They heaved it over one of the waist-high panels that formed a small pen, and poured the food into a covered feeder.

"There you go, boy," said Rebecca. "You can jump in here anytime, and those pesky ewes can't eat all your food."

She knew that, given the chance, the sheep would gobble up all Blizzard's food — they loved the salty taste.

Blizzard still felt like a puppy sometimes, and he was always excited to see Mrs. Hancock and Rebecca. He romped around his human friends, startling the sheep, who were not used to seeing him act this way.

Blizzard slid to a stop in front of Rebecca, who scratched him behind his ears. "I can hardly find his ears under all this hair," said the girl.

"We should groom Blizzard one of these days, Rebecca," Mrs. Hancock remarked. "We don't want his coat to get matted."

Blizzard was starting to develop the unique coat of the komondor. Komondors have been used to guard sheep and other livestock for hundreds of years in Hungary. The unusual coat serves as a sort of armor to protect the dogs from the wolves found there.

If Blizzard's hair was not allowed to mat as it grew, it would naturally form cords, or long strings. Rebecca knelt down and gently tugged on Blizzard's short cords so that the hair separated down to the skin. She knew that if she kept the cords separated, he would look like a canine string mop — just as a komondor should.

Blizzard loved to be groomed. The Hancocks did not fuss over him often. They wanted him to be loyal to the sheep, and not follow his human friends around. Rebecca stood and patted him on the head. "We'll work more on your coat soon, big guy," she told Blizzard.

"We've been hearing those coyotes at night, Rebecca," her mother said, "but so far they've been leaving our sheep alone."

"Last night at the 4-H meeting, I heard Danny Sullivan say that the coyotes had killed two lambs on their ranch," Rebecca said. "I hope Blizzard keeps those coyotes away from our sheep."

"He's a brave dog. I'm sure he's doing his best," Mrs. Hancock replied. "Speaking of 4-H, it's time for you to pick a lamb to show at the county fair. It will be here sooner than you think, and you have lots of work to do."

"I know, Mom," said Rebecca. It would be Rebecca's first year to show a lamb at the annual fair. She would have to raise the lamb — feed it, exercise it, train it to lead, and teach it to stand quietly for the judges. She knew that girls and boys in 4-H from all over the county would be doing the same thing. Each would be hoping to win a prize at the fair.

Rebecca looked over the lambs who were lying in the shade, but none of them seemed just right to her. "I can't decide," she told her mother.

Chapter 2

Ebony

Early the next morning, Rebecca's father, Dr. Hancock, and Panda, the Border collie, headed out to the pasture to gather the sheep and drive them to the barnyard corral. Dr. Hancock had a veterinary clinic in the nearby town, and he wanted to check the sheep closely and make sure all the lambs were doing well.

Blizzard was never too happy to see the black-and-white herding dog — and neither were the sheep. The sheep had learned that Blizzard was their friend, and they were not afraid of him. Panda, however, was a different story!

Panda's job was to round up the sheep when the Hancocks needed to move them or put them in the corral. He didn't bite the sheep — the Hancocks would never allow that — but he was very scary with his sharp eyes and quick movements.

The sheep gathered together and headed for the corral gate when they saw Panda coming. Blizzard trailed along with the flock, keeping his eye on the black-and-white dog the whole way in from the pasture.

Soon Dr. Hancock and Panda had the sheep in the corral. Mrs. Hancock closed the gate behind them. She stood for a moment and admired the ewes. They were very pretty in the morning sunshine with their black, brown, gray, and white fleeces. Their wool was just beginning to grow out from the shearing they had received earlier that spring.

The Hancocks raised sheep of many different colors because Mrs. Hancock used their fleeces to spin yarn and knit hats, mittens, and sweaters. She preferred to make patterns out of the natural colors instead of dyeing the wool. Mrs. Hancock imagined herself sitting in front of the spinning wheel, feeling the silky wool as it slid through her fingers and twisted into yarn.

She was startled out of her daydream by Rebecca's voice. "Mom," called her daughter, "there's a little black lamb over here in the corner. Why isn't she with her mother?"

Mrs. Hancock walked over to look at the lamb. She checked the lamb's eartag, which had been clipped into its ear for identification. She found that the lone lamb was one of a pair of twins.

"I don't think this lamb's mother has enough milk for two," Mrs. Hancock told Rebecca. "The other twin is stronger and is taking most of the milk. This one would do better if she were raised on a bottle, like Libby was."

Rebecca remembered that last summer she and her younger brother, Chad, had fed Libby and another lamb by hand.

Blizzard had been a puppy then, and lived with the lambs all the time.

Rebecca recalled how, twice a day, they had carried soda bottles to the pen where the lambs lived. The bottles were filled with a special milk formula for lambs, and topped by shiny black rubber nipples.

She knew that the little black lamb would soon learn to drink from a bottle, and would grow fat and healthy. Such lambs were called "orphans" or "bums," and already the Hancocks had two lambs that they were raising on bottles.

Rebecca had an idea. "Mom, may I take this lamb to the fair for my 4-H project?"

Mrs. Hancock thought it over. "Well, they do have a class for orphan lambs. I don't see why you shouldn't."

Rebecca shouted happily and scooped the fluffy black lamb up into her arms. The lamb looked at Rebecca curiously, as if to ask, "Who is this? Where is my mother?"

"I will call her Ebony," Rebecca declared, "Ebony Hancock."

Soon Ebony was settled in happily with the other two bum lambs. In addition to their bottles of milk, the three orphans were given grain pellets to help them grow. Rebecca took care of Ebony. Chad helped with the other two lambs.

Chapter 3

A Strange Disappearance

A few weeks later, Chad was sound asleep in his bed. It was early morning, with the sun just starting to rise. The sounds of bleating and barking woke him up. Chad got out of bed and ran over to his window. He could see a large bunch of sheep being herded up the nearby dirt road.

Chad knew that it was the time of year when the large range herds of sheep, numbering a thousand ewes and their lambs, were taken to the mountains. At the rear of the bunch of sheep, Chad could see two sheepherders. Sometimes they shouted to the dogs in Spanish: *"Venga!"* — Come! — or *"Detrás!"* — Get back! Most sheepherders, Chad knew, came to Wyoming from Spain, Mexico, or Peru.

From his bedroom window, Chad could see his family's flock, with their many shades of wool, grazing peacefully. Some of them were looking curiously through the fence at the passing herd. Chad saw Blizzard pacing watchfully, eyeing the strangers.

Chad noticed the three orphan lambs running around their pen in the barnyard. They could hear the strange sheep and were excited. *"Maa, maa,"* they called out to the passing strangers.

A short time later, Chad heard voices from the kitchen.

"Mom, Ebony and the other lambs are gone!" Chad ran to the kitchen to see Rebecca standing in the doorway, holding three full bottles of milk.

"The gate is open," Rebecca said. "I can't find the lambs anywhere!"

"Let's go look," Mrs. Hancock told her children. "They can't be far."

"Sheep like to be with other sheep,"

said Mrs. Hancock. "They're probably up in the pasture with the others."

Chad ran to get dressed. Rebecca put the lambs' bottles in the refrigerator to keep the milk fresh. When Chad returned, the three of them headed out the door.

Blizzard had been up much of the night. He had not heard coyotes howling, but there had been a lot of barking. The big dog was watchful — the passing herd had disturbed him. Some people allowed their dogs to run loose. These dogs formed packs and sometimes attacked wildlife, such as deer, and domestic livestock, like sheep.

When Blizzard heard Rebecca, Chad, and Mrs. Hancock coming, he trotted up to them.

"Blizzard, have you seen my Ebony?" Rebecca asked. "We can't find her." The three Hancocks searched through the sheep. The bum lambs were nowhere to be found. Where could they be?

Mrs. Hancock patted Blizzard on the head. She told him, "Good boy!" and, "Stay."

"Let's go look in the corrals," Chad suggested.

But they could not find the three lambs in the corrals. Chad and Rebecca even checked inside the barn and the shed, though the doors were closed.

"It's so strange," said Mrs. Hancock. "Even if the lambs managed to get out of their pen, why would they leave? Where would they go?"

All at once, Chad knew. "Mom!" he cried. "Early this morning I saw the Lazy H trail herd go by on their way to the mountains."

"That's right!" said Mrs. Hancock. "Why didn't I think of that? The lambs must have gone with them. Let's get in the truck and go check."

Chapter 4

The Runaways

Soon the three Hancocks were in the pickup truck, heading down the road. Just past a bridge where the road crossed a stream, they could see the Lazy H sheep-wagon, attached to another pickup, stopped under a tree. The sheepwagon was a sort of a cross between an old-time covered wagon and a modern camper. When the herd got to their summer pasture in the mountains, the herder would live in the wagon.

The sheep, each with a big red Lazy H brand painted on its back, were sipping water from the creek or resting quietly in the shade. They had been on the trail since early morning and would rest until midafternoon, when it cooled off. The

Hancocks could see the herder sitting on his horse a short distance away.

"Mom, why do those sheep have paint brands instead of eartags?" asked Chad.

"They put paint brands on sheep that run on the open range so it's easy for people to see to whom the sheep belong," she explained as the pickup stopped and they stepped out.

"Hola! What can I do for you?"

Rebecca and Chad looked up at a big man with black hair and a fancy handlebar mustache that curled up at the ends. "Carlos, meet my children, Rebecca and Chad. This is Carlos Gomez, the Lazy H camptender," said Mrs. Hancock. They each shook hands solemnly with the tall man.

Before her mother could say anything, Rebecca blurted out, "Have you seen Ebony? I mean our bum lambs — they're gone! Did they come with your sheep?"

Carlos looked at Rebecca kindly. "Well, *señorita,* let's look around."

They walked slowly up to a group of lambs who were playing on the bank of the stream. They were careful not to scare them. The lambs stopped romping and stared curiously at the approaching people.

Suddenly, three lambs burst out of the group and ran up to Chad and Rebecca. It was Ebony and the other two lambs! They were looking for their bottles of milk. They hadn't eaten since the night before and they were hungry.

Rebecca threw her arms around Ebony's neck and gave her a big hug. The lamb nuzzled her eagerly.

"Would those happen to be the lambs you are looking for?" Carlos asked Mrs. Hancock with a smile.

Soon the three runaways were stowed safely in the back of the pickup. Carlos invited the family into the sheepwagon for a cup of tea and some cookies. The wagon looked small from the outside, but it was surprisingly roomy on the inside. It had a bed under the window, with a table that pulled out from underneath. There was a bench along each side, which concealed more storage space. On one side of the door was a small woodburning stove, and on the other was a shelf with a bucket of water. A kerosene lamp was fastened to one wall.

"Come and visit us in the mountains this summer," the dark-haired man told them. "Bring your lambs, too."

"Why are you taking the sheep to the mountains?" asked Chad.

Carlos paused while he twirled the curly end of his long mustache. "Well, *muchacho*," said Carlos, "when they reach their summer pasture in the high country, they will have plenty of fresh grass and cool water for the summer months."

Chad liked being in the wagon, surrounded by the big bunch of sheep. "But how do you eat? Do you stay in the same place all summer?" he asked.

"I'm the camptender," said Carlos. "Every few days, I'll bring groceries to the herder and move the sheep camp to a new spot.

"The sheep never remain long in one place," he told them. "My boss says it's important to move the sheep onto fresh pasture. We need to keep the ewes from eating too much grass in one area. We want to be sure that there's plenty of feed left for the wild animals — the deer and elk."

Chad and Rebecca wanted to stay and hear more from Carlos, but their mother said, "Come now. We need to get home and feed these lambs." Soon, they were on their way.

Chapter 5

A Quick Repair

When Mrs. Hancock and the children arrived home, they eagerly told Dr. Hancock about their adventure. "I almost forgot," said Mrs. Hancock. "I need to make sure that Blizzard has enough food."

After the three lambs were returned to their pen, and Rebecca and Chad had fed them their bottles of milk, Rebecca and Mrs. Hancock headed up to the pasture.

Blizzard came trotting over when he saw his friends, and this time the silvery-gray yearling ewe, Libby, came with him. She nuzzled Rebecca.

"I can't believe that Ebony will be this big next year," Rebecca told her mother. "She's just a baby now."

"Yes," said Mrs. Hancock, "and you need to train her to lead with the halter, and practice showing her for the fair while she's still small." Mrs. Hancock fished around in her pocket until she found a piece of "cake," a compressed pellet of hay and grain. She gave it to Libby, who gobbled up the special treat.

"You start walking that way around the pasture and check the fence," Mrs. Hancock told Rebecca with a wave of her arm. "I'll go the other direction and meet you by the back gate."

Blizzard followed Mrs. Hancock a short way from where the sheep were grazing, then sat down and whined. He had come far enough and did not want to leave his charges. Mrs. Hancock looked at him and said, "Very good, Blizzard. You go back now."

Blizzard looked at Mrs. Hancock carefully, then trotted over to where Libby was lying in the shade. He lay down

beside her and put his head down. Soon he was fast asleep.

In the meantime, Rebecca was walking around the pasture fence. Her parents had taught her to look for breaks in the fence, or holes under it, where a sheep might get out or a coyote or dog might get in.

She knew her mother was walking from the other direction. In the back part of the pasture, there were lots of cotton-wood trees. Some of them had fallen down, and Rebecca had to climb over them as she checked the fence.

Soon Rebecca was at the gate where she was to meet her mother. The gate opened onto an old road. The road was no longer used, and it was blocked by fallen trees. Rebecca could see a gully where the old road had washed out. The path was still good for walking. Now it was mostly used by deer and other game animals. She knew that it eventually came out on the main road.

Rebecca noticed that the bottom part of the wire gate had come unfastened. The gate was still tight at the top, but it was loose and gapped open below. Just then, she heard her mother approach.

"Look, Mom," said Rebecca, "this gate has come loose."

Mrs. Hancock took a pair of fencing pliers out of her pocket. She grasped the loose ends of the wire and twisted them around until the gate was tight. "There," she said, "that will hold it for a while. Your father plans to repair the whole fence this fall before the snows come."

Rebecca and Mrs. Hancock headed back across the pasture to the house. Rebecca was eager to get started with Ebony's training.

Chapter 6

Ebony Gets Ready

Before Rebecca knew it, it was early August, and almost time for the county fair. She was pleased. She had worked with Ebony nearly every day, and now she did not even need to use the halter. The little ewe wanted to follow her everywhere.

Just the other day, Rebecca had tied Ebony to a post with the halter and carefully handpicked and combed all of the dirt and pieces of straw out of Ebony's black fleece. She had used a curry-comb — a round metal comb with dull jagged teeth. She was careful not to pull out any of Ebony's growing wool. She didn't wash Ebony, because that would

remove the lanolin, or grease, and make the wool feel stiff.

When Rebecca was satisfied that Ebony's wool was as clean and pretty as she could make it, she put a white cloth coat on her. Rebecca and her mother had made the coat just for the lamb. It had a hole for Ebony's head, and strings that tied under her belly.

"There," Rebecca told the lamb, "this will keep your fleece clean until the show at the fair." Ebony nibbled at the strings, but they were tied snugly.

The day before the show, Chad helped Rebecca get everything ready. They would leave early the next morning to take Ebony to the fairgrounds in town, which were in the county seat twenty miles away. Rebecca's father had built her a wooden "showbox" with a hinged lid. Into the box went all the supplies that Rebecca would need at the fair — a lamb halter, a currycomb, a clean soft rag, a bottle of black shoe polish for polishing Ebony's hooves, and a pair of hand-operated sheep shears, which looked something like a large pair of scissors.

Blizzard watched curiously from the other side of the fence. What was going on? He saw Dr. Hancock back the pickup truck, with its bright red rack, up to the shed.

Dr. Hancock put a bale of alfalfa hay and a sack of grain into the pickup bed. Next he loaded the showbox. He made sure that these things were pushed up against the back of the cab. Next, he and Chad secured a wooden panel in front of everything so that Ebony could not break into the sack of grain on the trip, eat too much, and get a bellyache.

Blizzard paced back and forth. He hoped that no big changes were coming up. He did not like it when things were different.

Chapter 7

The Attack

The Hancocks had gone to bed early since they planned to leave first thing in the morning to go to the fair. All was quiet on the ranch, but Blizzard was restless.

He was standing under a tree in his favorite spot. Libby was asleep nearby. The other ewes and their lambs had settled down hours ago for the night. The moon cast a bright light over the sleeping flock. Now it was almost morning, and the pale dawn was just beginning to show in the east. Blizzard could see shadows from the trees rippling as a light breeze ruffled their branches.

Suddenly, the hairs on the back of Blizzard's neck stiffened. In the distance, he could hear the baying of dogs in a pack.

Blizzard stood up, growling low in his throat. He could hear the dogs very clearly now. He gave a loud warning bark. The sheep woke up, and the ewes bleated with alarm as they checked to see if their lambs were safe. Nervous, the sheep got up and moved closer together.

All at once, four dogs burst out of the shadows, running toward the terrified sheep. The ewes, calling their lambs, broke and ran toward the far end of the pasture, the bells around their necks ringing wildly. Blizzard sprang toward the leader of the pack, a large German shepherd.

The German shepherd was not as large as Blizzard, but he was older, and an experienced fighter. The intruder was surprised to find a dog among the sheep, but he soon gathered his wits.

Blizzard grabbed the back of the attacker's neck, and brought the German

shepherd to the ground. In the next instant, the wily dog twisted away and closed his teeth at Blizzard's throat. But instead of flesh and the jugular vein he was seeking, the dog's teeth met with the heavy leather collar Blizzard always wore.

The shepherd lunged again. This time he came away with a mouthful of hair. What sort of dog was this? Blizzard seemed to be all leather and fur.

The other three dogs in the pack had paused when Blizzard jumped on their leader. Soon, two of them took off again after the fleeing sheep. The fourth dog, a terrier, decided to join the fight. Blizzard succeeded in throwing the shepherd back, but before he knew it the terrier was barking and nipping at his face.

Blizzard grabbed the smaller dog by the back of the neck, gave him a rough shaking, and tossed him aside. He lay still where he landed, his neck broken. The shepherd was soon back on his feet, growling a deep menacing growl.

Blizzard could see the other dogs — a medium-sized black mutt and a large fuzzy dog — racing through the herd, biting and nipping the backs and hind legs of the sheep. The leaders were fleeing down the old road toward the gate. The air filled with the jangling of bells as the panicked sheep ran headlong toward the trees. It was growing lighter, as the sun started to rise, but the shadows were deep in the woods.

Blizzard was frantic. The shepherd lunged at him again, but Blizzard's size was a match for the older dog's experience.

Suddenly, a rifle shot rang out. The German shepherd sprang to his feet and raced toward the woods. Blizzard heard another shot as his opponent disappeared into the brush. He caught a glimpse of the other two dogs as they veered away from the sheep and fled with the German shepherd. The shots had frightened the loose dogs away.

Chapter 8

A Sad Day

Blizzard turned to the spot where he had last seen the sheep. He saw Dr. and Mrs. Hancock running toward the old road. Dr. Hancock was carrying a rifle. Blizzard plodded over toward the Hancocks. They stopped, and Dr. Hancock pushed the body of the terrier with the toe of his boot.

"This one is dead," he said to Mrs. Hancock, "but the other one got away."

"Look at Blizzard!" Mrs. Hancock exclaimed. "I think more than one got away."

Hunks of Blizzard's coat had been torn away and were hanging down in ribbons. Even though it was a mess, his thick komondor coat had protected him from injury.

Blizzard hung his head. He hurt all over, and he felt that he had failed in his job of protecting the sheep from harm. Mrs. Hancock petted his head and told him, "You're a good boy, Blizzard. You did your best." The dog brightened a bit at the kind tone of her voice.

Dr. Hancock gave Blizzard a quick examination. "He seems to be all right," he told his wife. "His coat sure is a mess, after all Rebecca's grooming. He looks like a pretty ragged komondor now. Let's go see if any sheep are hurt."

They started down the old road, with Blizzard following along behind them. It was now full light, with the morning sun showing above the horizon.

It didn't take long for them to find the first sheep. Terrified lambs were crying for their mothers. One lamb lay dead. Soon the Hancocks found a ewe with her leg badly torn. They could see the raw red muscle where the flesh had been ripped away.

The sad group followed the old road to the gate. They saw that the fleeing sheep had pushed into it and pulled away the wire where Mrs. Hancock had fixed it. It hung askew. In the woods, they could hear the sheep calling out, and the sound of bells. Without the dogs in pursuit, the sheep had slowed down and were milling around in the trees.

"Blizzard, stay," commanded Mrs. Hancock. Reluctantly, the white dog sat down near the gate. Dr. and Mrs. Hancock headed off in different directions to find the scattered sheep and bring them back to the pasture.

The Hancocks searched through the woods. They found the sheep by listening as the ewes called out for their lost lambs. They could hear the animals picking their way through the thick brush. Soon they had located most of the ewes and their lambs. They walked around and gathered the sheep into a bunch, then herded them down the old road to the gate.

A number of the ewes had patches of wool pulled out, but none were hurt as badly as the injured ewe in the pasture. Dr. Hancock picked up a lamb who had broken his leg in the fence, and he cradled the little creature in his arms.

"I don't know what's worse," he told his wife. "Coyotes hunt down the sheep, but they are wild creatures. These dogs aren't hungry. They just do it for sport."

"I wish people would keep their dogs tied up," said Mrs. Hancock. "I suppose they can't believe that their pets would deliberately tear up animals like this."

The Hancocks put the sheep back in the pasture. Blizzard watched as they counted them. After they added in the dead lamb and the injured ewe and lamb, they were still one short. "Who's missing?" Dr. Hancock asked his wife.

Blizzard walked through the exhausted flock. They eyed him warily, then relaxed a bit when they recognized him. He snorted with alarm. Where was Libby?

Chapter 9

Making Plans

"Should we put the sheep in the corral?" Mrs. Hancock asked.

"Yes," her husband answered. "I don't think those dogs will be back today, but it would be safer to leave the sheep in. They need to settle down."

Dr. Hancock used a sturdy stick as a splint for the lamb's broken leg. He pushed the bone into place and held it while Mrs. Hancock wrapped the leg and the splint firmly with special tape. They put the little lamb in a pen with her mother, so she wouldn't try to follow the ewe around.

"Let's go up to the pasture with the pickup and get the hurt ewe," Dr. Hancock told his wife. "She might get better if I treat her injuries."

After taking care of the sheep, the Hancocks headed back to the house. Rebecca and Chad were still sound asleep. They had missed all the uproar.

Over breakfast, Dr. and Mrs. Hancock explained what had happened. Rebecca and Chad were upset, especially about the dead lamb.

Chad wanted to stay to search for Libby, who was still missing, but his parents told him that they must first take Rebecca and her lamb into town for the fair. "Rebecca and Ebony have been getting ready all summer," Mrs. Hancock pointed out. "We can't let her miss the show."

"I'll tell you what, Chad," Dr. Hancock said. "After we take Rebecca to the fair, you and I will stop at my clinic in town. We'll need to get some medicine for the ewe and lamb that were hurt, then you and I will come back and look for Libby."

He turned to Rebecca. "Rebecca, I'm sorry, honey. Will you feel bad if Chad and I miss the show?"

"Oh, no! I want you to come back and find Libby," Rebecca cried. "I want to show Ebony, but I'm sorry it's today. I wish I could help you look."

Rebecca and Mrs. Hancock went to the lamb pen and got Ebony. The lamb trotted along behind Rebecca and followed her over to the pickup. Mrs. Hancock lifted her into the back of the pickup. Rebecca closed the tailgate, then closed the gate on the rack.

"Whew!" exclaimed Mrs. Hancock. "Ebony's grown a lot. She's sure a good eater."

In the meantime, Chad and Dr. Hancock were taking care of the rest of the sheep. They put some hay into the feeder and made sure the water tank was full.

"We'd better tie Blizzard, I think," said Dr. Hancock. "He had a rough time, and I don't want him running off looking for Libby."

Chad couldn't find Blizzard's chain, so he got a thick rope and gave it to his father. Dr. Hancock tied one end of the rope to Blizzard's collar and the other to a corral post. "That should do. We won't be gone too long."

Blizzard watched sadly as the pickup headed down the driveway and out of sight. He couldn't understand why everyone had left. Why were the sheep in the corral? Why had he been tied up? Most important, where was his friend Libby?

Blizzard let out a howl. The sad sound echoed across the pasture to the woods. He howled again and again. The sheep watched him carefully. They had never seen him act so strangely.

Chapter 10

Off to the Fair

In spite of her worries about the missing ewe, Rebecca was excited as the pickup jolted along the dirt road. The cab was crowded, and Chad kept bouncing into her lap whenever they hit a bump. Normally she would have complained, but she was too excited today to gripe at her brother.

Soon they were on the highway. Rebecca kept looking out the rear window to check on Ebony. Of course she knew Ebony was still there, because the lamb kept up a steady bleating. Was Ebony wondering why she was being taken away from her friends in the bum lamb pen? She didn't seem to like being alone one bit, and she didn't care for the strange ride, either!

Finally, they reached the fairgrounds on the edge of town. Dr. Hancock backed the pickup up to a wooden loading chute. Rebecca opened the gate on the rack and unfastened the tailgate on the back of the pickup. Dr. Hancock lifted out the little ewe. Rebecca fished the halter out of the showbox and fitted it over Ebony's head. She did not want her lamb to get scared and run off! She led Ebony toward the sheep barn, while her dad lugged the showbox.

"What did you put in here — rocks?" asked Dr. Hancock good-naturedly.

In the meantime, Mrs. Hancock and Chad went to the nearby sheep barn and located Ebony's pen. It was fun greeting all their old friends from around the county, and admiring the livestock. In no time Rebecca had Ebony safely in her pen. She scattered sawdust on the pen's dirt floor so that Ebony would have clean bedding, and brought her a bucket of fresh water.

All around they could see other families unloading animals — horses, cattle, and hogs — and sheep of all types. Each species had its own barn. There was even a building where poultry and rabbits were on display. The fair would last for several days, but the lamb show was to be that very afternoon.

It was all Dr. Hancock and Chad could do to tear themselves away from the fair, but they knew they'd better get the medicine and return home to doctor the injured sheep. Chad was anxious to find Libby. Dr. Hancock didn't mention his fears to his family, but he knew that the young ewe might very well be dead.

Dr. Hancock hugged Rebecca and wished her luck. Even Chad told Rebecca that he hoped Ebony would win a prize. He was a bit jealous because he was still too young to join 4-H. Next year he could enter.

Chapter 11

Lamb Chops and Ram-bo

Mrs. Hancock and Rebecca decided to take a look around the sheep barn before the show started. There were lots of "market lambs" that had been fattened over the summer for the show. They would be judged for their quality as meat producers.

The market lambs, mostly blackface breeds like Hampshires and Suffolks, had been sheared down almost to the skin and washed so that they practically gleamed. Rebecca's friend Allison was putting the finishing touches on her market lamb. She was on her hands and knees.

"Hi, Allison," called Rebecca. Her friend twisted around and looked up at

Rebecca. "What are you doing on the ground?" Rebecca didn't see much of Allison when school was out, so she was glad to talk to her.

"I'm just putting black shoe polish on Lamb Chops' hooves so he'll look nice," said Allison. "What did you bring?"

"I have an orphan lamb, Ebony," Rebecca told her. "She is small, but she has the nicest black fleece you've ever seen."

"I have a bum lamb, too," said Allison. "Her name is Shoshone. But she's a Hampshire like Lamb Chops, so she's sheared, too."

Mrs. Hancock came over to the girls. "Come on, Rebecca. I want you to see these beautiful fleeces on the Rambouillets."

Rebecca knew that Rambouillets were an all-white breed of sheep that had originally come from France. In the United States, they had been especially bred into big sheep with fine, strong wool. Many flocks of range sheep, like those on the Lazy H, were of Rambouillet breeding, and they supplied wool for fine woolen clothing.

Rebecca waved good-bye to Allison and followed her mother to the other side of the barn. She gasped when she saw the size of the Rambouillet ram in a pen in front of her. He had a huge set of horns that curled from the sides of his head. The sign on his pen said RAM-BO.

Mrs. Hancock was soon visiting happily with Ram-bo's owner, who was going to show the big ram and several ewes in the Open Class, for adults. The fine Rambouillet fleeces were harder to spin than the coarser wool of the Hancocks' colored sheep, but they made a beautiful, slender thread. Soon Mrs. Hancock bargained for the purchase of a couple of fleeces the next spring, following shearing.

Rebecca and Mrs. Hancock toured the rest of the barn and admired the other wool-type sheep, such as the Columbias and the Targhees. These sheep were shown in their fleeces, and their owners were busily clipping the wool smooth with hand shears.

The only other colored sheep at the show besides Ebony belonged to Jeb Roberts, the Hancocks' neighbor. The Roberts family had bought their ram from the Hancocks, and he was the father of Jeb's lamb.

Rebecca knew that most sheep who have colored fleeces are from white-wooled breeds. Occasionally a lamb with a colored fleece is born to a white ewe, just as sometimes a redheaded baby is born to brown- or blond-haired parents. Colored sheep, though, are more likely to have black, brown, or gray lambs.

"Mom, I'd better get Ebony ready. I hope she can win a prize!" Rebecca exclaimed. The sight of everyone busily preparing their sheep made her eager for Ebony to look her best. She knew the competition would be tough.

Chapter 12

Libby Trapped!

Blizzard was unhappy. He could see the sheep in the corral. They looked safe enough, but he could sense that the ewes were nervous. The mothers wouldn't let their lambs out of their sight. They were bleating anxiously and nosing the lambs to reassure themselves.

Blizzard kept sniffing in the direction of the sheep. Where was Libby? If he were not tied up, he could check to see if she was there. He was pretty sure she wasn't. He *had* to do something.

Blizzard lay down and began gnawing at the rope. It was a thick one, but it was soft and old. In a short time he had gnawed through most of the rope. Only a few strands held it together. Just then he heard a ewe *maa-ing* frantically. He jumped up and ran toward the ewe. As he reached the end of the rope, the remaining rope fibers snapped, and he was free.

Blizzard trotted into the corral to locate the frightened mother, but she had found her straying lamb and was quiet. The big dog sniffed through the sheep, checking them. They had settled down and seemed to remember their old friend. Libby was nowhere to be found.

Blizzard was confused. He knew his job was to stay with the bunch, yet he also knew Libby should be with them. Should he leave the flock to search for her? Maybe he'd just go a little way.

Blizzard jumped out of the sheep pen and went to investigate the other corrals. He trotted around, but there was no sign of his friend. He even checked the bum lamb pen, but only the two orphans were there, lying in the shade.

Blizzard walked slowly out to the near

part of the pasture. He still had a good view of the sheep pen, so he went on a little farther. Soon he found himself on the old road that led out to the gate. Now he began trotting faster, leaving the barnyard behind. He could smell the disturbed ground where the sheep had run during the dog attack. The gate was still down.

Blizzard stopped and checked around. Not far away, he heard a bark. The sound came from down the fenceline, in an area of thick brush. Blizzard let out a large warning "Woof!" and ran toward the noise.

There was silence for a moment, then the barking resumed. Blizzard crashed through the thick brush and practically ran over an ugly-looking mutt. It was the black dog who had run away!

The mutt backed away, but behind him was the mean German shepherd. There was no sign of the fuzzy dog. On the other side of the dogs was Libby. In her

panic, she had run right into the fence, and her head was stuck through one of the squares in the woven wire. She was trapped!

The mutt was a bully, but he knew that Blizzard was a larger, stronger dog. He did not intend to challenge the big dog. The German shepherd, however, felt that their previous fight had been unfinished. He meant to take care of the big white dog this time.

Chapter 13

Showtime

In the meantime, at the fair Rebecca was waiting for her class to be called. The market lamb classes were nearly done. After the Grand Champion market lamb was picked, the orphan lamb class would be next.

She looked around at the other lambs. They were a very mixed group. The lambs ranged from large meaty animals to small scruffy ones. She was glad to see how round and healthy Ebony had become on her diet of milk, grain, and fresh grass.

"Grand Champion market lamb is shown by Allison Hanson," announced a voice over the loudspeaker. Rebecca cheered for her friend. She had been so busy grooming Ebony that she had not watched the class in the ring. She saw Allison and Lamb Chops receiving a huge purple ribbon and a big shiny trophy. She hoped Ebony could win such a prize!

"4-H orphan lambs, enter the show ring," came the announcement. Rebecca gave her black lamb a quick hug. She slipped off Ebony's halter. Halters were not allowed in the show ring.

Even though Ebony would have followed her like a puppy, Rebecca put one hand on the lamb's tail and the other under her chin. She expertly guided the lamb into the show ring, making sure to keep the lamb between herself and the judge. She and Ebony had practiced many times at home, with Mrs. Hancock acting as the judge.

Rebecca lined up Ebony next to the other lambs, and carefully placed the lamb's feet squarely under her. She recalled her mother's words: "Make her look like a table, with a leg under each corner."

The judge was walking up and down the row of sheep. Orphan lamb classes were hard to judge, he knew, because many different types of sheep were shown. It was hard to compare a meat-type lamb to a wool-breed lamb or to a ram lamb who was to be kept in the flock.

After examining each lamb carefully, he finally walked over to the microphone. "It's clear," he announced, "that all of you have worked very hard to raise these lambs without their mothers. You've done an excellent job, and I commend you. I am only going to name a Champion and a Reserve Champion. The Reserve Champion orphan lamb belongs to Allison Hanson."

Rebecca tried to be happy for her friend, but it didn't seem fair that Allison should get *two* major prizes! The judge announced the Champion, who belonged to a boy from the other side of the county whom Rebecca hardly knew.

Rebecca and the other youngsters guided their lambs out of the ring while the Champions received their prizes and trophies. There was even a photographer from the newspaper there to take their photos! Both lambs were meat-type lambs — one Hampshire and one Suffolk.

Rebecca was haltering Ebony and trying not to look disappointed when another announcement came over the loudspeaker. A woman's voice said, "Following the breeding sheep show, the County Wool Growers Association is sponsoring a special class for wool sheep. We want to encourage spinning and other fiber arts, and the class will be judged on that basis. Entries will be taken at the judge's table."

Rebecca headed for the barn. She put

Ebony's coat back on her to protect her fleece. She found Allison and congratulated her. She really was glad her friend's lambs had won prizes, if Ebony couldn't be the winner.

Chapter 14

Chad to the Rescue

Chad and Dr. Hancock had not wasted any time. They had picked up the supplies from the vet clinic and headed directly back to the ranch.

It seemed like the trip back took a long time. Both Dr. Hancock and Chad were worried about Libby. They knew that most of the dogs from the pack had gotten away and might come back.

The truck pulled into the barnyard, and Dr. Hancock and Chad got out. "Here, Chad, put this penicillin into the refrigerator while I check the sheep and untie Blizzard."

Chad did his job, then ran to join his father at the sheep corral. He found Dr.

Hancock examining the frayed end of Blizzard's rope.

"I can't believe Blizzard would run off and leave the ewes," Dr. Hancock told his son. "I thought he knew better than that."

Dr. Hancock headed to the barn. "Let's get the hand shears and clip some of this pulled wool. Then we can see how much damage the dogs did, and we can clean the wounds."

"Dad," said Chad, "I'm worried about Libby. Can I go walk around the pasture and see if I can find her?"

"Okay, son, but don't go far. Come and get me if you find anything," Dr. Hancock replied. "And don't be gone long."

Chad headed out into the pasture. His father hadn't mentioned it, but he was old enough to know that he might not find Libby alive.

As Chad headed to the far end of the pasture, he heard barking. Chad recognized Blizzard's bark. He started running toward the sound, and soon realized that he was on the old road that led out of the gate. He didn't want to go much farther, but he had to see what the commotion was about.

Chad went through the gate and stopped to listen. On the other side of a thick patch of brush he could hear barking and growling, but it sounded like more than one dog. He climbed along the fence to avoid the heavy brush.

First Chad saw Libby, her head stuck through the wire and frozen in terror. Just behind her stood Blizzard, growling fiercely at the German shepherd. As Chad watched with alarm, the German shepherd sprang at Blizzard. The mutt, watching from the brush, sensed two dogs could beat Blizzard. He came running out of the brush, ready to join the fight.

Chad knew better than to get into the middle of a dog fight, but he had to do something! He picked up some rocks and began hurling them at the mutt. The first rock missed, but the next two connected and sent the ugly dog running. Chad didn't think he'd be back.

Chad didn't know what to do next. If he ran to get his father, it might be too late for Libby and for Blizzard. The fighting dogs looked like a blur, and if he threw rocks he might hit Blizzard. Chad looked at Libby. She was trying to get away from the fight, but was only succeeding in getting herself more stuck.

Chad jumped down to the pasture side of the fence. He grabbed Libby's head and began pushing. At first, she was stuck because strands of her wool were caught in the wires. Chad twisted her head slightly, and suddenly she popped free.

Libby was so frightened that she made another lunge forward, but luckily she hit the wire and bounced back. She saw an opening in the brush and bounded through it. She headed for the gate.

Chapter 15

A Fierce Fight

Dr. Hancock finished snipping the wool away from the ewe who had been bitten the most. He would have to stitch her loose skin.

He was heading to get a bucket of warm soapy water to clean the ewe's wounds when he stopped. "Maybe I'd better check on Chad," he said to himself. "He's been gone a long time." He grabbed his rifle, just in case.

As Dr. Hancock strode through the pasture, he saw Blizzard's food pen. He couldn't understand why Blizzard had left the sheep. The dog had been trained to stay with them.

"Chad," called Dr. Hancock. "Chad!"

Just then, Dr. Hancock heard a noise. He saw Libby running full tilt down the old road. She swept past him in the direction of the barn. He was relieved to see her alive, but wondered what had frightened her so.

When Dr. Hancock reached the gate, he could hear sounds of the dog fight on the other side of the brush. He pushed along the fenceline and found a scared-looking Chad, holding a rock and watching the fierce fight.

The German shepherd had Blizzard down, but he couldn't get a good grip on the hairy white dog. Suddenly Blizzard gave a mighty heave and threw the shepherd backward. A shot rang out, and the pack leader fell dead.

Blizzard sniffed at the limp body. Moments earlier, the German shepherd had been at his throat.

"Dad! Blizzard is bleeding," cried Chad.

"What about you, son?" asked Dr. Hancock. "Are you all right?"

"I'm okay," said Chad, though his heart was pounding. They examined Blizzard, who had a nasty bite on his leg.

"I think he'll be all right, but we'd better take him into town to the clinic. What happened?" Dr. Hancock asked.

Chad told the story, including how he had frightened the black dog away by throwing rocks.

"You showed good judgment, son," said Dr. Hancock. "You freed Libby, you kept two dogs from ganging up on Blizzard, and most important, you had the good sense to stay out of the dog fight. I don't think that other dog will be back. This one was the leader."

Dr. Hancock and Chad looked at the dead dog at their feet. The dog wore a collar, and he was obviously well fed, so he belonged to someone. They checked the collar but couldn't find any tags. Dr.

Hancock shook his head. "All because some people let their dogs run loose!"

Both Chad and Blizzard looked exhausted. Dr. Hancock said, "Let's go, boys. There's nothing more we can do here."

Chapter 16

A Happy Ending

"Rebecca, you'd better get Ebony ready to show. They'll be starting in a few minutes."

Startled, Rebecca looked at her mother. Surely her mom knew she had already been in the Orphan Lamb Class. Rebecca had even seen her taking pictures!

"What do you mean, Mom?" asked Rebecca. "We're all through."

"Why, you and Ebony are entered in the fleece sheep contest." Mrs. Hancock smiled at her daughter. "She has a pretty fleece. You should hurry to get her ready."

Rebecca was surprised. She'd been so

disappointed, she'd hardly listened to the announcement about the fleece sheep contest. She jumped off the edge of Ebony's pen, where she'd been sitting, and found the lamb's halter. "Come on, Ebony," she said. "Let's show everyone how pretty you are."

Soon, Rebecca and Ebony were once again lined up in the show ring. About half a dozen other lambs were there as well, mostly Rambouillets.

The judge carefully examined each lamb. Rebecca didn't take her eyes off him. She moved from one side of Ebony to the other. She took care that the judge always had a good view of her lamb and that Ebony always stood squarely. All their hours of practice were paying off!

The judge pulled a tuft of wool from each lamb and examined it carefully. He tugged each tuft firmly to check its strength. Finally he motioned three lambs

forward — Rebecca's, Jeb's, and a beautiful white lamb.

For what seemed like an eternity, the judge studied the three lambs. He looked directly at Rebecca. She swallowed hard and smiled. Her mom had always told her to look like she was having fun, but how could she when she was so nervous?

The judge walked over to the microphone. "This class is a tough one," he said to the onlookers. "When I consider the quality of the fleeces, especially for hand spinners, I have to look at qualities such as strength, cleanliness, and the length of the wool.

"I have decided that the white lamb out there will be my Reserve Champion, and the black lamb will be the Champion," he continued.

Rebecca heard cheering. She looked up and saw her mother, father, and Chad. Her father was waving to her to come forward. Suddenly she realized that the black lamb was Ebony, and she had won first place!

The next thing Rebecca knew, she was holding a trophy and a stuffed toy lamb donated by the County Wool Growers. She gave Ebony a big hug, and just then a flashbulb went off. It was the photographer from the local newspaper!

When they returned to the barn, Rebecca fed Ebony. Chad came in carrying a bucket of fresh water and set it down in the pen.

"What are you guys doing here?" Rebecca asked. "What about Libby?"

Chad told her the story of Blizzard's escape and the search for Libby. "After Dad finished stitching the injured ewe, we decided to leave the sheep in the corral for the day," Chad said. "We brought Blizzard to Dad's clinic."

"To the clinic!" exclaimed Rebecca. "What's wrong with Blizzard?"

"He'll be fine," Dr. Hancock spoke up.

"I needed to bring him in so I could treat his leg where that German shepherd bit him."

"We thought you'd be all done at the show," Rebecca's father continued. "Chad and I were pretty surprised to see you getting a trophy."

Chapter 17

Brave Dog Blizzard

Blizzard sniffed the air and looked around. All the ewes were grazing peacefully. Occasionally, an anxious mother would bleat, then settle down when she located her lamb. The lambs were romping, but they were close by. Already a few yellow leaves were beginning to show in the cottonwood trees, and the sheep were enjoying one of the last summer days.

Blizzard lay down. Libby was nearby. The only reminder Blizzard had of their adventure was a sore leg, but he was feeling better every day.

He heard voices. It was Mrs. Hancock and Rebecca so he only raised his head. What was that behind them? Now he jumped up. There were three lambs!

"Here you go, Ebony," said Rebecca. "You may be a Champion, but it's time for you and your friends to join the other sheep."

The three bum lambs watched as Mrs. Hancock and Rebecca headed back toward the barnyard. They looked startled when they saw Blizzard. Who was this giant? The big dog ambled over and sniffed noses with the lambs. He wanted them to know that they were welcome, and that he would take care of them.

About the Author

Sharon Salisbury O'Toole lives in Wyoming, where this story takes place, with her husband and three children. She is a writer and a sheep rancher and has written many articles about sheep for adults.

This is Mrs. O'Toole's second story for children. Her first book, *Noodles, Sheep Security Guard*, was also about a Hungarian komondor. The komondors in Mrs. O'Toole's stories are modeled after a real dog that she trained to guard the sheep on her ranch, and who became the sheep's best friend and a beloved member of the family.

LITTLE 🍎 APPLE

BABY·SITTERS

Little Sister™

by Ann M. Martin, author of *The Baby-sitters Club* ®

☐	MQ44300-3	#1	Karen's Witch	$2.75
☐	MQ44259-7	#2	Karen's Roller Skates	$2.75
☐	MQ44299-6	#3	Karen's Worst Day	$2.75
☐	MQ44264-3	#4	Karen's Kittycat Club	$2.75
☐	MQ44258-9	#5	Karen's School Picture	$2.75
☐	MQ44298-8	#6	Karen's Little Sister	$2.75
☐	MQ44257-0	#7	Karen's Birthday	$2.75
☐	MQ42670-2	#8	Karen's Haircut	$2.75
☐	MQ43652-X	#9	Karen's Sleepover	$2.75
☐	MQ43651-1	#10	Karen's Grandmothers	$2.75
☐	MQ43650-3	#11	Karen's Prize	$2.75
☐	MQ43649-X	#12	Karen's Ghost	$2.75
☐	MQ43648-1	#13	Karen's Surprise	$2.75
☐	MQ43646-5	#14	Karen's New Year	$2.75
☐	MQ43645-7	#15	Karen's in Love	$2.75
☐	MQ43644-9	#16	Karen's Goldfish	$2.75
☐	MQ43643-0	#17	Karen's Brothers	$2.75
☐	MQ43642-2	#18	Karen's Home-Run	$2.75
☐	MQ43641-4	#19	Karen's Good-Bye	$2.75
☐	MQ44823-4	#20	Karen's Carnival	$2.75
☐	MQ44824-2	#21	Karen's New Teacher	$2.75
☐	MQ44833-1	#22	Karen's Little Witch	$2.75
☐	MQ44832-3	#23	Karen's Doll	$2.75
☐	MQ44859-5	#24	Karen's School Trip	$2.75
☐	MQ44831-5	#25	Karen's Pen Pal	$2.75
☐	MQ44830-7	#26	Karen's Ducklings	$2.75
☐	MQ44829-3	#27	Karen's Big Joke	$2.75
☐	MQ44828-5	#28	Karen's Tea Party	$2.75
☐	MQ44825-0	#29	Karen's Cartwheel	$2.75
☐	MQ43647-3		Karen's Wish Super Special #1	$2.95
☐	MQ44834-X		Karen's Plane Trip Super Special #2	$2.95
☐	MQ44827-7		Karen's Mystery Super Special #3	$2.95

Available wherever you buy books, or use this order form.

Scholastic Inc., P.O. Box 7502, 2931 E. McCarty Street, Jefferson City, MO 65102

Please send me the books I have checked above. I am enclosing $_____ (please add $2.00 to cover shipping and handling). Send check or money order - no cash or C.O.Ds please.

Name_____

Address_____

City_____ State/Zip_____

Please allow four to six weeks for delivery. Offer good in U.S.A. only. Sorry, mail orders are not available to residents to Canada. Prices subject to change.   BLS991